Dear Parents,

Our world is filled with letters—those magical squiggles and lines we see on signs, in books, almost everywhere we look. Helping your child unlock the mystery of these squiggles can get him or her on the right track to reading success.

One way to lay the foundation for early reading success is reading to and with your child every day. **Step into Reading Phonics** books offer a unique way to turn daily reading into a pleasant and valuable experience. These books are designed to help your child learn about the sounds that letters stand for, how letters come together to make words, and how words can be put together to make sentences. They contain controlled text that introduces children to words they will see often in early reading books. Engaging illustrations help your child see the connection between words and pictures.

Begin by reading this book aloud to your child. As you read:

- Point to each word. This "tracking" of the print will help your child make a connection between the written and spoken word.
- Emphasize the sounds in rhyming words, such as *cat* and *hat,* or words that share a common consonant, such as *sand* and *silly.*
- Talk about the pictures on each page. Then say a word from the text and have your child find it. You can give hints, such as "This word starts with the /s/ sound" or "It rhymes with *cat.*"

When your child feels comfortable with the story, have him or her read it to you, a friend, or even a pet! Praise your child's efforts and encourage rereading of the story. Invite your child to find words from the story on signs or in other books. This will generate excitement about and interest in words.

Remember—all children deserve the gift of reading. As parents, you can help bestow that gift. Whatever you do, have fun with this book and instill the joy of reading in your child. It is one of the most important things you can do!

Wiley Blevins, Author and Reading Specialist
Ed.M., Harvard University

For Andrew
—A.J.H.
To Super Sosha and Silly Bob
—S.W.

Text copyright © 2002 by Anna Jane Hays.
Illustrations copyright © 2002 by Sylvie Wickstrom.
All rights reserved under International and Pan-American Copyright Conventions. Published in the United States by Random House, Inc., New York, and simultaneously in Canada by Random House of Canada Limited, Toronto.

www.randomhouse.com/kids

Library of Congress Cataloging-in-Publication Data
Hays, Anna Jane.
Silly Sara / by Anna Jane Hays ; illustrated by Sylvie Wickstrom.
p.   cm. — (Step into reading. Step 1 book)
"A phonics reader."
Summary: Alliterative rhyming tale of a girl who can be very silly but with her best friend, Sam, she discovers she can be something more.
ISBN 0-375-81231-8 (trade) — ISBN 0-375-91231-2 (lib. bdg.)
[1. Clumsiness—Fiction. 2. Best friends—Fiction. 3. Stories in rhyme.] I. Wickstrom, Sylvie, ill. II. Title. III. Series.

PZ8.3.H3337 Si 2002
[E]—dc21
2001019285

Printed in the United States of America   First Edition   January 2002   10 9 8 7 6 5 4 3 2 1

STEP INTO READING, RANDOM HOUSE, and the Random House colophon are registered trademarks of Random House, Inc.

Silly Sara

A Phonics Reader

A Step 1 Phonics Book

by Anna Jane Hays

illustrated by Sylvie Wickstrom

Random House 🏠 New York

Sara sat on a sofa.

She sipped a smoothie.

OOPS!

The smoothie spilled.

Silly Sara.

Sara sat in the tub.

She licked a lollipop.

PLOP!

The lollipop dropped.

Silly Sara.

Silly Sara sat

on her hat.

Silly Sara tripped
on her cat.

Silly Sara slipped
on the mat.

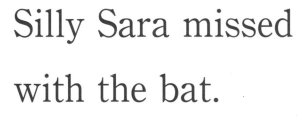

Silly Sara missed
with the bat.

Sara chewed
bubble gum.

She blew a big bubble.

Then a bigger bubble.

Then the biggest bubble.

Silly Sara.

The door went SLAM!

In came Sam.

"You have a funny face."

"Hey, want to race?"

Sam and Sara

scooted fast.

Sara was first.

Sam was last.

Speedy Sara!

Sam and Sara played
hide-and-seek.
Sara had to peek.

"Eek!"

Sara saw Sam.

Sam and Sara sat
on a seesaw.
They licked ice cream.

Sandy stepped on.

Sara went up.

Sara's ice cream

fell down.

SLURP!
Sandy found it
on the ground.

Sara had a hunch
it was time for lunch.

Sara had jam.

Sam had ham.

Which?

Sara and Sam had
a jam ham sandwich.

Sam gobbled up his
jam ham sandwich.

"I am Super Sam!"

he said.

"Now <u>you</u> have

a funny face," said Sara.

"Don't be silly, Sara."

"Okay," she said.

"I am not Silly Sara."

"I am <u>Super</u> Sara!"

"And we are super pals!"